Sofie and the City

Sofie
and the City

Karima Grant

Illustrated by **Janet Montecalvo**

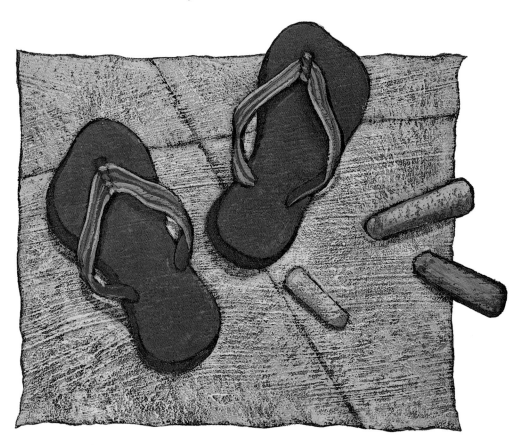

Boyds Mills Press
Honesdale, Pennsylvania

Boyds Mills Press, Inc.
A Highlights Company
815 Church Street
Honesdale, Pennsylvania 18431
Printed in China
www.boydsmillspress.com

Library of Congress Cataloging-in-Publication Data

Grant, Karima.
Sofie and the city / by Karima Grant ; illustrated by Janet Montecalvo.— 1st ed.
   p. cm.
Summary: When Sofie calls her grandmother in Senegal on Sundays, she
complains about the ugliness of the city she now lives in, but her life changes
when she makes a new friend.
ISBN 1-59078-273-9 (alk. paper)
[1. Immigrants—Fiction. 2. City and town life—Fiction. 3. African Americans—Fiction.
4. Friendship—Fiction. 5. Senegal—Fiction.] I. Montecalvo, Janet, ill. II. Title.

PZ7.G76677553Sof 2006
  [E]—dc22   2005020116

First edition, 2006
The text of this book is set in 14-point Caxton Book.
The illustrations are done in acrylic.

10 9 8 7 6 5 4 3 2

For the Mames: Sokhna Diallo, Mareme Sene,
Marie-Anne Cisse, and Lee Young;
For the Abbotts, with all my love: Daddy, Sousou, Momo, and baby Edou;
And, of course, their Meme and G. G.

—K. G.

To Mom and Dad, for never doubting that I could do it

—J. M.

Chum!
   Sofie sticks her nose up at the ugliness here.
   The new city has hard gray sidewalks that poke fun at brown feet wearing plastic flip-flops from Senegal. Buildings filled with people stretch nearly to the sky.

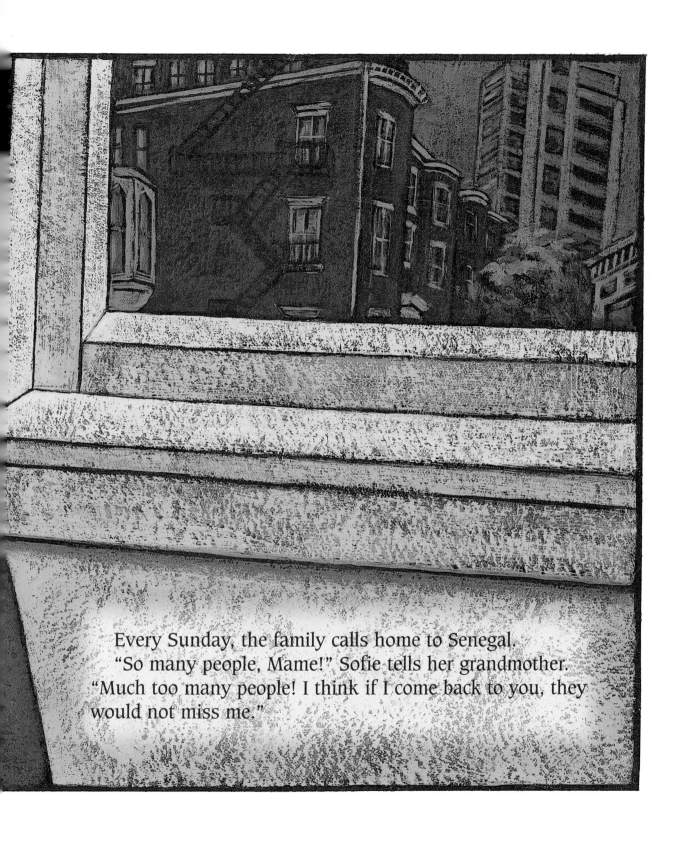

Every Sunday, the family calls home to Senegal.
"So many people, Mame!" Sofie tells her grandmother.
"Much too many people! I think if I come back to you, they
would not miss me."

Sofie's mother works the long days braiding hair. It is almost dinnertime when she returns home, tired. Then it is Papa's turn to leave and drive the big yellow taxi through the dark and noisy night.

"Maman sleeps during the night," Sofie tells Mame.
"Papa during the day! I think if I come back to Senegal,
they will not notice."

Sofie counts in English the twenty-eight stairs to her stoop where she sits and watches the city go by.

Although it is summertime, the city is cold. Although the sun is bright and day has begun, nobody calls to her.

Nobody waves from the passing cars or buses.
Nobody plays music for her to dance to. Nobody listens
to her practicing her very best English.

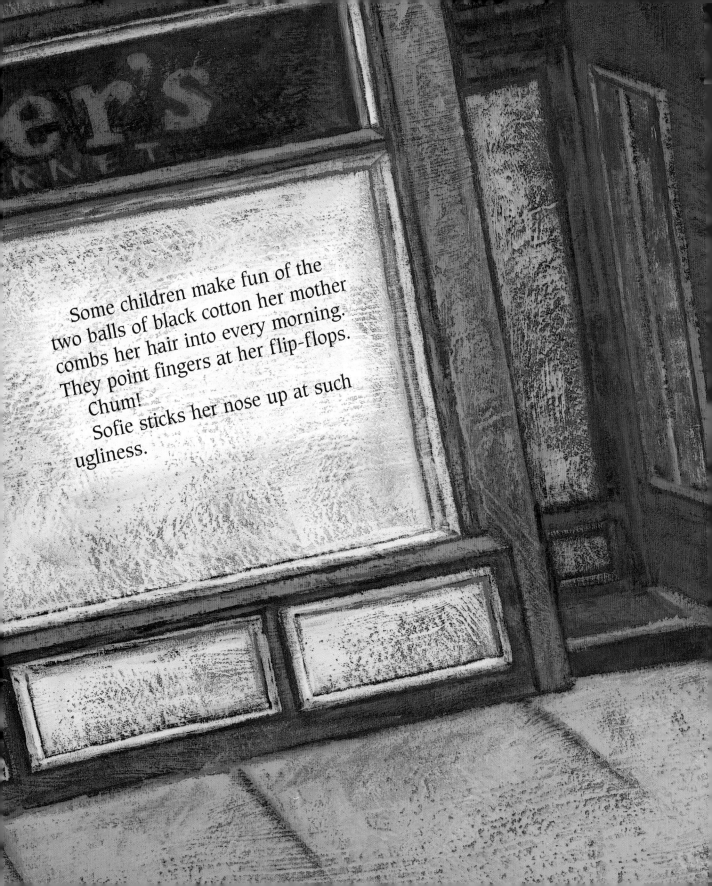

Some children make fun of the
two balls of black cotton her mother
combs her hair into every morning.
They point fingers at her flip-flops.
Chum!
Sofie sticks her nose up at such
ugliness.

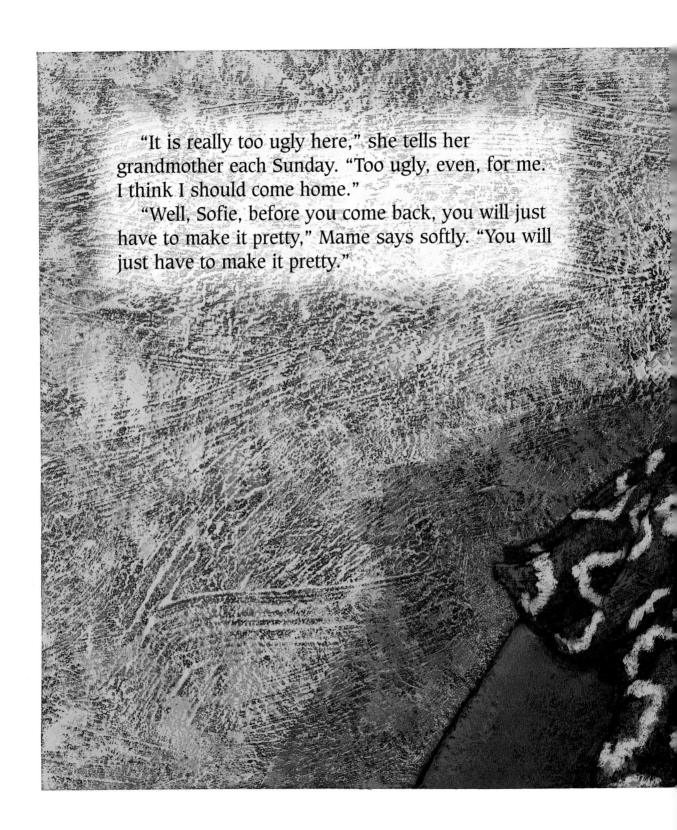

"It is really too ugly here," she tells her grandmother each Sunday. "Too ugly, even, for me. I think I should come home."

"Well, Sofie, before you come back, you will just have to make it pretty," Mame says softly. "You will just have to make it pretty."

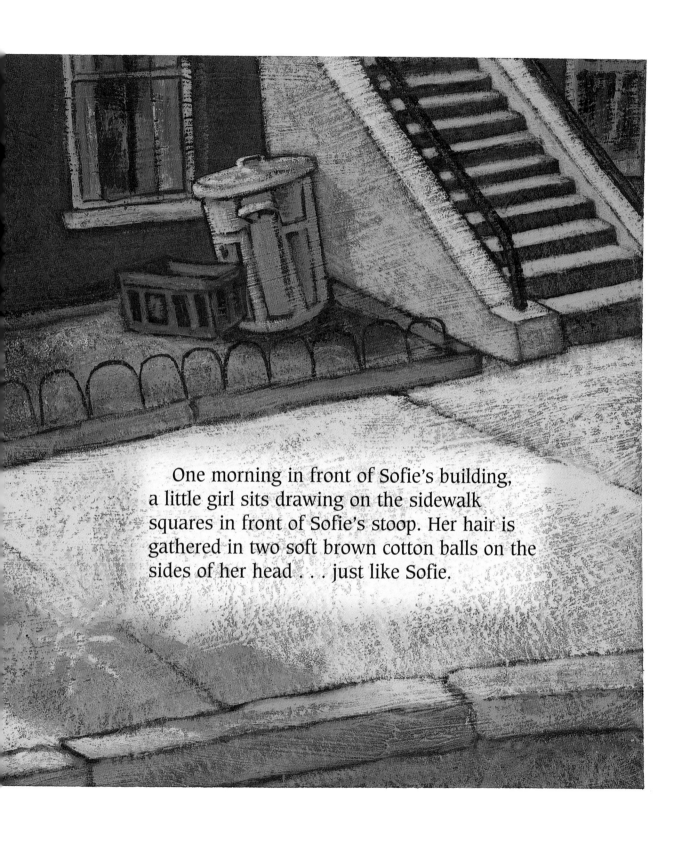

One morning in front of Sofie's building,
a little girl sits drawing on the sidewalk
squares in front of Sofie's stoop. Her hair is
gathered in two soft brown cotton balls on the
sides of her head . . . just like Sofie.

Sofie walks over to the little girl,
who is writing letters in different colors.
   "What is that?" asks Sofie, forgetting that
her voice sometimes makes funny sounds when
she is speaking English.
   "My name," says the little girl. Sofie reads the
letters aloud.
   "Ken-ya . . ."
The little girl smiles proudly.

Sofie takes the purple chalk and spells out her name. "So-fie . . . ," reads Kenya. "My name," says Sofie proudly.

Sofie sees that Kenya has covered the sidewalk in sparkling color.

"What is that?" Sofie asks.

"That is my city," says Kenya. She points to the tall buildings, the rushing taxis, and the many, many people she has drawn, all smiling at Sofie.

Sofie takes the blue chalk and kneels against the hard cement.

From her chalk pours the sea, blue and curving.
On it swim the painted pirogue boats of the fishermen.
Along the shore in yellow, Sofie colors in the warm
sand that always kissed brown feet in plastic flip-
flops. On the sand, Sofie draws her grandmother,
laughing and waving.

"What is that?" asks Kenya.

"My home . . . ," says Sofie.

That Sunday, Sofie tells her grandmother about Kenya, who shares her chalk.

"Together we color the ground every day, Mame!"

"And what do you draw, Sofie?"

"Sometimes we draw home, sometimes we draw here," says Sofie. "But always we write our names."

"And do you still want to come back, Sofie?" asks Mame.

"It is not so ugly here anymore. It has become very pretty, actually. I think I will be missed if I go home."

Mame's laugh is low and long. Sofie imagines her grandmother's head-wrap slipping backward.

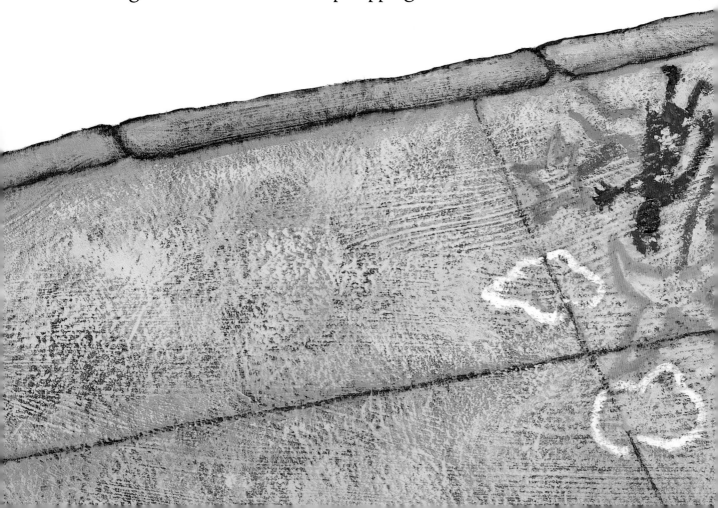

"Yes," agrees Mame. "I think you will be missed, too."